Taylor is a children's author, storyteller and teacher. His books The Great Snake, the *Purple Class* series, and the multi-award winning a Monster is Born. Both *Crocodiles are the Best Animals of All Purple Class and the Half-Eaten Sweater* were shortlisted for the Roald Dahl Funny Prize 2009. Sea es partly in England and partly in Brazil where his wife is from. www.seantaylorstories.com

Hannah aw graduated from Brighton University with a BA in illustration. nce then she has worked as a freelance illustrator, author and graphic designer, but has also worked in a chocolate shop and factory. She currently lives in a tiny village in Gloucestershire with Ben the blacksmith and Ren the dog. www.hannahshawillustrator.co.uk

For Ameya, Sam and Tim – ST
For Will and Joce – HS

Crocodiles are the Best Animals of All copyright © Frances Lincoln Limited 2009
Text copyright © Sean Taylor 2009
Illustrations copyright © Hannah Shaw 2009
The right of Sean Taylor and Hannah Shaw to be identified respectively as the author
and illustrator of this work has been asserted by them in accordance with the Copyright,
Designs and Patents Act, 1988 (United Kingdom).

First published in Great Britain and in the USA in 2009 by
Frances Lincoln Children's Books, 4 Torriano Mews,
Torriano Avenue, London NW5 2RZ
www.franceslincoln.com

First paperback published in Great Britain in 2010

A catalogue record for this book is available from the British Library.

ISBN 978-1-84780-132-6

Illustrated with pen and ink and scanned textures
Typeset in Later On

Printed in Dongguan, Guangdong, China
by TOPPAN Leefung in October 2009

1 3 5 7 9 8 6 4 2

CROCODILES ARE THE BEST ANIMALS OF ALL!

by SeAN tAYLoR

iLLUStRAteD bY HANNAH SHAW

F

FRANCES LINCOLN
CHILDREN'S BOOKS

A donkey gave a nod of his head.

He chewed a bit and then he said,

"My ears may wiggle and my teeth may be wonky,

but nothing is better than being a donkey!"

"I AM BETTER!" came a loud boast.
"I could eat you for breakfast with buttered toast!"

Up came a crocodile, swimming front crawl.
He said, "**CROCODILES ARE THE BEST ANIMALS OF ALL!**"

He did it without a slip or a fall,

hissing,

"CROCODILES ARE THE BEST ANIMALS OF ALL!"

"I nibble grass and seedlings and shoots!

I even chomp up Wellington boots!"

He nibbled towards them with a growl and a call, "CROCODILES ARE THE BEST ANIMALS OF ALL!"

A mountain goat did not agree.

He said,
"You can't climb as well as me!"

"Pish Posh!" said the crocodile. "I can climb
And play the bongos at the same time!"

He clambered a mountain until he looked very small,

shouting, "**CROCODILES ARE THE BEST ANIMALS OF ALL!**"

He bounced about like a basket ball, chuckling,

"CROCODILES ARE THE BEST ANIMALS OF ALL!"

The crocodile grinned. He had won the day.
But then he heard the donkey say,

"You're good at many things, I can see,

but you cannot wiggle your ears like me."

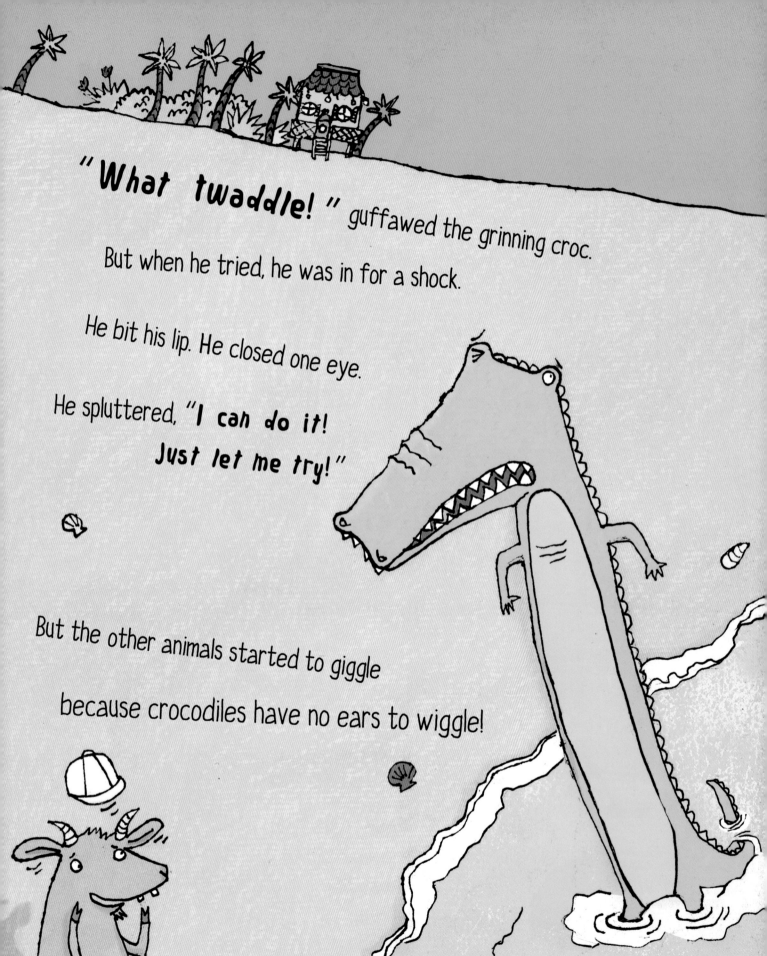

"**What twaddle!**" guffawed the grinning croc.

But when he tried, he was in for a shock.

He bit his lip. He closed one eye.

He spluttered, "**I can do it!
Just let me try!**"

But the other animals started to giggle

because crocodiles have no ears to wiggle!

The donkey gave a nod of his head.

He chewed a bit and then he said,

"My ears may wiggle and my teeth may be wonky,

but **nothing is better** than being a donkey!"

MORE TITLES FROM FRANCES LINCOLN CHILDREN'S BOOKS

Number Rhymes: Tens and Teens
Opal Dunn
Illustrated by Hannah Shaw

Make numbers fun with this entertaining collection of rhymes specially chosen by an expert early childhood language. With its wonderful humorous illustrations, this companion to Opal Dunn's very successful *Number Rhymes to Say and Play* is another delightful and valuable aid to developing early numeracy skills.

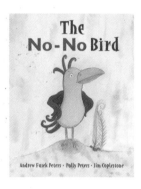

The No-No Bird
Andrew Fusek Peters and Polly Peters
Illustrated by Jim Coplestone

No-No Bird's favourite word is NO!
He says NO to everyone and NO to everything.
Then he meets Snake and learns that Snake's favourite food is No-No Bird. Can No-No Bird escape a sticky end by changing his favourite word to YES?

Down the Back of the Chair
Margaret Mahy
Illustrated by Polly Dunbar

When Dad loses his keys, toddler Mary suspects they are down the back of the chair.
Join in the fun as the family search and find everything from a bandicoot and a bumblebee to a string of pearls and a lion with curls. But will it be enough to save the family from rack and ruin?

Frances Lincoln titles are available from all good bookshops.
You can also buy books and find out more about your favourite titles, authors and illustrators on our website: www.franceslincoln.com